Camp Zombie
The Second Summer

by Megan Stine and H. William Stine

BULLSEYE CHILLERS™

RANDOM HOUSE 🏠 NEW YORK

To Cody's friends—
Adam, Akilah, Daniel, Elliot,
Gabe, Lauren, Lela, and Nat

A BULLSEYE BOOK PUBLISHED BY RANDOM HOUSE, INC.

Text copyright © 1995 by Megan Stine and H. William Stine.
Cover illustration copyright © 1995 by David Henderson.
All rights reserved under International and Pan-American Copyright Conventions. Published in the United States by Random House, Inc., New York, and simultaneously in Canada by Random House of Canada Limited, Toronto.

Library of Congress Cataloging-in-Publication Data:
Stine, Megan.
    Camp Zombie : the second summer / by Megan Stine and H. William Stine.
      p. cm. — (Bullseye chillers)
    SUMMARY: When his parents drop him off at camp, eleven-year-old Griffen Alexander realizes that he feels uneasy about staying because it is the same camp that his cousins went to last year—the place they called Camp Zombie.
    ISBN 0-679-87075-X (pbk.)
    [1. Monsters—Fiction. 2. Camps—Fiction. 3. Horror stories.]
I. Stine, H. William. II. Title. III. Series.
    PZ7.S86035Cap 1995 [Fic]—dc20 94-67466

Manufactured in the United States of America 10 9 8 7 6 5 4 3 2 1

Chapter 1

The moment I set foot on the grounds of Camp Kennebec, I got jolted by this strange feeling. Like somehow I'd been there before.

Calm down, Griffen, I told myself. It's just your imagination.

But I couldn't calm down. There was something weird about the place. It gave me the creeps.

"We've got to go," my mom said, looking at her watch. "We've got to catch our plane."

I glanced at my watch. It was only 7:00 A.M.

"You're kidding," I said. "You're leaving me here? Alone? At seven in the morning?

This place is deserted!"

"The counselors are all eating breakfast," my mom said. "They'll be out soon. Anyway, this gives you a chance to look around before anyone else arrives."

Right, Mom, I thought. That's any kid's dream come true. Being dropped off at camp before *any* kids get there.

"Besides," my mom went on, "you've already met the camp director, Mr. McDonald. So you're not really alone."

Oh, right. Me and my buddy, Mr. McDonald.

As I thought about him, I got that creepy feeling again. Like I had heard his name somewhere before.

I didn't like the looks of McDonald. He had a really fake smile.

I gave my mom a pleading look. It didn't work.

"We've *got* to go, Griffen," she repeated.

"Okay," I finally said, trying to sound like it was no big deal. "See ya."

My mom gave me a big hug. So did my dad. Then they left me standing there on the porch of my cabin. Cabin 5. Even that seemed familiar to me.

I looked out at the trees and down toward the lake.

The lake...I thought to myself. I'll bet it's long and shaped like a hot dog bun.

But how did I know that? I hadn't ever been here before. Or had I?

The creepy feeling washed over me again, like a chilly blast of air in a restaurant when the air conditioner is blowing too hard. It was so strong, I wanted to run after my mom and dad and beg them to take me with them.

But I didn't do it. I knew they'd never give in.

And anyway, I'd been really excited about going to camp—until we got there. I mean, it was the first time in my eleven years that I'd been out of New York City for more than a week.

So here I was, Griffen Alexander, the only kid at Camp Kennebec. It felt like I was the only kid in Maine.

I went back into my cabin and looked around. What a mess! The inside was just nailed-up board walls, board floor, and board ceiling. It was really grungy, too. They hadn't even bothered to paint it.

The main room was pretty big, but there was a lot of empty space. There were just three wooden bunk beds with plank shelves beside each one.

My sleeping bag and duffel were still on the bed where I'd tossed them earlier. But I didn't feel like unpacking yet.

So I went outside to look around. Tall pine trees surrounded the cabin on three sides. I checked out where everything was—the showers, the baseball field, Mr. McDonald's office, stuff like that. Everything looked pretty run-down—except for the large dining hall. It was brand-new. I could still smell fresh paint when I walked by it. Too bad the whole camp wasn't new.

Then I went down to the lake. I was right about the lake—it *was* shaped like a hot dog bun! And there was a floating dock out in the middle.

Creepy, I thought. Something bad happened in this lake. I just know it.

Across the lake I saw a lot of dark log cabins. I could hear voices, too.

What's over there? I wondered. Another part of Camp Kennebec? I figured it wouldn't take too long to find out. So I started to walk around the lake. But a voice stopped me.

"Hey, yo! Where are you going?"

I turned back and saw a muscular guy about twenty years old. He was jogging toward me. His Camp Kennebec T-shirt was sweaty.

"You can't hike around the lake by yourself," he said, taking deep breaths as he jogged in place.

"Why not?" I asked.

"Beats me," he said. He smiled and pushed his sunglasses up on top of his curly black hair. "I'm a new counselor this year so I don't know why. McDonald says that's the rule. And he was real clear about it—nobody goes alone."

"Oh," I said, looking again at the cabins across the lake.

"I'm Dave, Cabin 4," he said.

"Griffen," I said. "Cabin 5. Hey, what's over there, anyway?"

"Another camp. A boys' camp," Dave explained. "We'll play baseball against them at the end of the session. You like baseball?" He motioned toward my New York Mets cap.

"Yeah," I said.

"Good. Well, see ya around," he said, jogging off again.

"Yeah, sure," I said.

"And stay away from Camp Black Bear," he called back to me.

Camp Black Bear? As soon as I heard the

name, I started getting that feeling again. Like I'd heard it somewhere before.

Then it hit me. Like a punch in the stomach.

Camp Black Bear? Wasn't that the camp my cousin Corey went to last summer? The one with the *zombies?*

Suddenly I remembered. No! Black Bear was the camp *across the lake* from the camp Corey went to!

All at once I knew why everything—the camp, the lake, Mr. McDonald, and Cabin 5—seemed so familiar to me.

"Oh no!" I cried out loud. "I know where I am. I'm *at* Camp Zombie!"

Chapter 2

Camp Zombie. The words made me shudder. That's what Corey had called it. And his sister, Amanda, too. She had come here with him last summer.

I tried to remember everything they'd told me. But it was hard. Because when Corey had talked about the zombies, I thought it was a joke.

I wasn't laughing now. Something told me it was all true. Every word he'd said.

I looked around for a place to sit down and think. There was a small dock near shore. A rowboat was tied up to it.

Okay, I'm at the same camp, I told myself. That's why everything seems so familiar. Because I've heard about all of this before.

Thanks, Mom and Dad. Great choice of camp.

But am I really afraid of zombies?

I mean *really*. Zombies?

They didn't exist. They couldn't. No way. Except one thing kept bothering me. Corey and Amanda never lied. They were the two most honest people I knew.

I don't know how long I sat there, trying to remember things Corey had told me. When I finally looked behind me, I saw that the camp was starting to fill up. Lots of kids were hauling their stuff up to the cabins. Some were even playing ball already.

I wondered what was going on in my cabin. Were my cabin mates there yet? There was only one way to find out.

I hurried back to Cabin 5 and stood outside it for a minute. Metal music came booming out the door. Guys were laughing in there, too.

Well, this was it. Time to meet my cabin mates.

Do or die, I told myself as I walked in.

No one even looked up when they heard the screen door bang.

"Hi," I said to the five guys sprawled all over the cabin.

They ignored me. Every single one of them.

One guy was doing push-ups.

The other four had to be tight friends, because they were all dressed alike. They all had on the same Chicago White Sox hats and T-shirts. And big baggy plaid shorts that came down below their knees.

One of them was playing a Game Boy. The other three were going around the cabin taping White Sox posters on the walls.

I swallowed hard. I couldn't believe it. What a nightmare! I was rooming with American League fans!

Finally, one of them stopped putting up posters and turned to stare at me. As soon as he did, the others did, too. They turned down the metal music. Then they all stared at my New York Mets cap.

The leader seemed to be a skinny red-haired kid with a million freckles.

"Are you from New York?" he asked. He made it sound like a crime.

"Yeah. So?" I said.

One of his friends snickered and mumbled, "What a Larry."

Then they all started shoving each other and laughing.

Larry? What were they talking about? It didn't make any sense.

"My name's Griffen," I said.

The red-haired kid looked up at me with a mean stare.

"We moved your stuff, New York," he said. Then he grinned. Like he knew he had just slapped me with a nickname that would stick forever.

I looked over at my bunk. My stuff was gone, all right.

"Where?"

"In there, New York." He pointed to a

door on the far side of the cabin. It was some kind of room, but it had been locked when I first got there.

"Don't touch my stuff again," I said. Then I marched to the door, pushed it open, and walked right in.

Uh-oh, I thought. Big mistake.

Standing in the middle of the room was a guy who was about twenty years old. He looked as surprised to see me as I was to see him. He was a little short and pudgy for his age. I could tell because he was standing there in nothing but his red polka-dot boxer shorts. He had a gray mouse in each hand and another mouse on top of his head. It peeked out at me through the guy's dirty blond hair.

"Uh, are my bags in here?" I asked.

I could hear laughter in the room behind me. The White Sox fans had tricked me. Now they were going crazy.

"Close the door!" the mouse man said. "I told those guys not to come in here without knocking first."

I closed the door, but not before giving my cabin mates a look that said I'd deal with them later.

"You could have ruined my whole experiment," the mouse man said. He grabbed the mice and put them back into their cages. All together, he had about a dozen small animal cages. They were stacked up on a wooden desk.

"Are you the exterminator?" I asked. It was a lame joke. But I couldn't figure out what else to say. I mean, what was he doing with all those mice?

"I'm Lance," he said, holding out his hand. "I'm your counselor."

I really wanted him to wash his hand before I shook it.

"Have you ever seen a gecko?" he asked.

Before I could answer, he started telling me all about the animals in his room. Most of them were mice, but he also had a snake, a gecko, a guinea pig, and a frog. It was some sort of college science experiment.

Finally, about ten minutes later, he remembered we were at camp, not college.

"By the way, do you have any questions?" Lance asked.

Questions? You bet. Like why was I in a cabin with five jerks? And what did my roommates do with my stuff? And were there really zombies at this camp? And, if there were, what happened to the last zombie—the one my cousins called Brian?

But Lance didn't look like he could answer questions about anything except mice.

So I said, "When do we eat?"

"I don't know," answered Lance. "I think they ring a bell or something."

Oh, brother, I thought. I closed Lance's door behind me as I left. This was going to be a long three weeks.

The four Chicago guys were still laughing. But at least they had put my stuff back on my bed.

Not the bed I had picked out, though.

The crummiest bed in the room. The bottom bunk in the corner with no window.

In an hour or so, the lunch bell rang. By then I was starving. So we all marched down to the dining hall by the lake for our first meal together.

The White Sox guys walked together. I walked with the other guy, whose name was Raphael. He was the one who had been doing push-ups when I walked in. He still hadn't said a word to me.

As soon as we got to our table, the kid with the red hair—his name was Craig— unscrewed the top of the salt and pepper shakers. But he left the tops on, so they looked normal. That way, the tops would fall off when you tried to put salt on something.

Craig punched his buddy Elliot, and they both burst out laughing.

"Totally Larry," said Elliot.

Totally obnoxious, I thought.

The four of them called everything

"Larry." They thought it was cool. But I thought it was just about the only word they knew.

Then Craig poured half a glass of water into the ketchup bottle.

"Wait till Lance asks for the salt. Or the ketchup," Craig said. He grinned at Elliot and his other two friends, Nat and Julian.

A few minutes later, Lance sat down with a tray of food. He reached for the ketchup and poured it on his home fries. It gushed out of the bottle, covering his plate, his shirt, and his pants.

I knew I should be laughing. It was a pretty funny joke. But I took one look at Lance, and all I could think of was blood.

Like a zombie had taken a bite out of him.

No doubt about it—I had zombies on the brain.

For the rest of the day, I wanted to tell my roommates about the zombies. But I didn't get a chance until later that night.

Ten o'clock. Time for lights out.

I lay in my sleeping bag on top of my bunk mattress. The room was dark, darker than any room I'd ever seen. It *never* got this dark in New York City. There are too many lights. Even my *closet* at home wasn't this dark.

Anyway, Lance was gone, so the place was really quiet. He had gone to a counselors' meeting in the dining hall. I could hear the eerie creak of his mice running on their exercise wheels. It was really creepy.

"Somebody tell a ghost story," said Craig. "It'll be funny. Nat barfs when he gets scared."

"Shut up, you Larry," said Nat, sniffing up snot. He was always sniffling. He had bad allergies.

They wanted a ghost story? I had one they'd never forget! Here was my big chance.

"I'll tell you a story," I said. "It's a real killer."

Chapter 3

"Okay. Let's hear your Larry story," Craig said.

Everyone got quiet.

I sat up and rested my back against the wall in the dark.

"I have two cousins, Corey and Amanda. They live in Ohio," I said.

"Heard it," interrupted Elliot.

Of the four Chicago guys, he was the worst. Always the first one to mouth off and the last one to listen. He was short, with black hair and glasses.

"You haven't heard the best part," I said. "Because I'm the only one who knows it."

"Ooooh—I'm *so* scared," Elliot said.

The other guys laughed. Except Raphael

in the bunk above me. He never talked. He hadn't said a word to anyone the whole day.

I waited for them to stop laughing. Then I went on with my story.

"Last summer Corey and Amanda went to a summer camp," I said. "It was called Harvest Moon. Cabins, trees, a lake, a ball field—it looked just like a regular camp. But it wasn't. It had been closed for twenty years...because of all the accidents."

"What kind of accidents?" Craig asked.

I smiled in the dark. I'd been dying to tell this story all day. Now someone was finally listening.

"Twenty years ago, five people all disappeared in the camp lake," I said.

"You mean they drowned," said Craig.

"No," I said. "*Disappeared*. People *thought* they drowned—but they never found the bodies. Even though they searched the whole lake."

"How come?" Nat asked.

I lowered my voice so that they'd have to

be quiet to hear what I said next.

"It was something in the lake," I said. "Something under the dock. It pulled them under, kept them down there, and turned them into zombies."

"Right. Zombies. I really believe that," said Elliot.

"Do you want to hear the story or not?" I asked.

"Shut up, Elliot," Craig said.

I took a deep breath. "As soon as Corey and Amanda got to camp, the zombies started coming out. One night they stole the meat from the kitchen. Then they tried to eat a kid—one of Corey's cabin mates. After that, no one was safe. Not in the woods. Not in the lake. Not after dark."

"What happened to your cousins?" Raphael asked quietly from the bunk above me. "Did they die?"

It was the first nice thing anyone had said to me. And the first time he had talked. I smiled again.

"No, my cousins got away," I said. "Five zombies chased them all the way across the lake and into the dining hall. Then, by accident, the building caught fire and the zombies burned up."

"Cool," Raphael said.

It was quiet for a second. Then I heard Nat nervously slap his bed.

"Nice try, New York," Elliot said. "But you didn't make Nat hurl his dinner—he's not even gagging. So it looks like your story was a flop."

"You haven't heard all of it yet," I said.

"Oh, yeah?" Craig said. "What else?"

"I forgot to tell you that the camp Corey and Amanda went to was in Maine. Same as Camp Kennebec. And Camp Harvest Moon's dining hall burned down—and we have a brand-new one. Their camp director's name was McDonald. So is ours." I saved the best for last. "And the boys' camp across the lake was *Camp Black Bear*. Just like here."

"Hey, wait a minute," Nat asked. His

voice shook. "Are you saying this is the *same* camp?"

"Yeah," I said. "The very same camp—with a new name."

Nat squirmed nervously in his bed. "But all the zombies got fried in the fire, right?"

"No, they didn't," I said.

"What?" Julian said in a high voice. He was the youngest of the Chicago guys. He was smaller than all the others, too.

"Five zombies burned up in the dining hall," I said. "But Corey told me there was a sixth one. His counselor."

"Yo! His counselor was a zombie?" asked Raphael.

"Not at first. At first he was just a lowlife with a mean streak," I said. "His name was Brian, and he was really mean to Corey. He always wore a Raiders cap. One night, Brian rowed across the lake and disappeared. When he came back, he was a zombie."

"Yeah, sure," Elliot said quickly. "There's no such thing as a zombie."

"But what if it's true?" I asked. "If it is, it means Brian is still out there somewhere. Waiting."

"It can't be true," Craig said. "Because if it is, it means McDonald knows all about this zombie stuff. He'd have to. He was here last year, right? He owns this camp. And what kind of a camp director would keep a camp open with a bunch of zombies running around?"

"A crazy one," I said. "That's what Corey told me."

Nat sniffed up in the dark, and I thought I heard him gag. Like he was going to barf.

"I know it sounds unbelievable," I said. "I didn't believe it either. But how come everything Corey told me is true about Camp Kennebec? Tell me that?"

No one answered for a long time. So I swung out of my bunk to get a drink of water. My throat was suddenly dry. I walked across the creaky, rough wood floor to the other end of the cabin.

When I got to the tiny bathroom, I felt for the light switch inside the door.

Nothing. I couldn't find it. I kept feeling around on the wall, but it wasn't there.

Oh well, I thought. There's enough moonlight coming in the window to get a drink.

I groped my way to the sink and ran the water into my cupped hands. Then I put my face down close to the sink and slurped the water up.

But after a few gulps, I noticed something. A strange rotten smell was floating toward me. Coming in from the window at my side.

Yuk, I thought. Something stinks. I looked up at the screened window—and nearly jumped out of my skin.

There was someone standing outside—looking in!

I sucked in my breath and stepped back. "Who's out there?" I said, my voice shaking with fright.

The person was tall and stood stiffly, leaning his head toward the window. With the moonlight behind him, all I could see was the shadow of his face pressed against the window screen. He didn't move.

I grabbed for a flashlight that hung by a rawhide string on the wall. Finally I found it and fumbled to turn the thing on.

When the light hit him, he backed away from the screen. And that's when I saw his face—his twisted, gray face. His spongy skin looked like it was sliding off his skull.

Then I saw his eyes—dead eyes. Eyes that never blinked, never moved. He was wearing a torn and dirty black cap. But even though it was caked with mud, I could still see the silver Raiders symbol on it.

All at once my heart jumped straight into my throat. I knew the person staring in at me wasn't dead or alive. He was a zombie. It was Brian!

Chapter 4

"AAAHIIII!" I screamed, so hard I thought I'd wake up the whole camp. My eyes were locked on the hideous creature staring back at me through the bathroom window.

Instantly, the other guys came running and pushing into the small bathroom. Nat and Craig had their flashlights on.

"What? What's wrong?" Craig asked, shining his light in my eyes.

"The window," I gasped, pointing.

They aimed their flashlights toward the screen. But it was empty. Nothing was there. No one blocked the view into the night.

"Never see a window before?" Elliot

asked with a mean chuckle.

"It was him. Brian. The zombie," I said. My voice was still jumpy. "He was standing there, looking in."

Elliot cocked his head sideways. "New York, do you have a medical problem or are you just totally weird?" he asked.

"I'm telling you the *truth*," I said, getting angry. "I saw someone outside!"

"What did he look like?" asked Nat.

"He was wearing a cap—a *Raiders* cap!" I said. "And he had really dead-looking eyes."

"Okay, maybe there was someone there," Craig said, leaving the bathroom. "But it wasn't a zombie. Probably a counselor walking night patrol. They check the cabins every hour."

"Jeez," Elliot said as he followed Craig out. "Haven't you ever been to camp before?"

"No," I admitted, going back to my bunk and sitting on the edge.

"You mean you've never been away from home for even one itty-bitty night?" Elliot taunted me.

"No," I said again. "But I know what I saw. It was Brian."

"Don't think so," Craig said.

"Me neither," Elliot said. Then he changed the subject. "So who's for sneaking out tonight—to do some damage? I say we go scare the girls. Or at least toilet-paper their cabins."

"What's that?" Julian asked in his high voice.

"Toilet-paper," Elliot snapped. "You know. Trash their cabin with rolls of toilet paper. So they have to clean it up in the morning."

"Cool," Craig said. "I'm up for it."

"Uh, I don't know," Nat said. "Sneak out on the first night? We don't even know our way around." He sounded nervous.

Craig shined his flashlight down into Nat's bunk. "What's the matter?" Craig said. "You *scared* of the big bad zombie, Natty-boy?"

"No way," Nat said, trying to sound brave.

"Okay, then," Craig said. "We're doing it. I mean, we've got to show this Larry camp that Cabin Five rules, right?"

"For sure," said Elliot, turning on his flashlight and crossing beams with Craig.

"Are you coming, Julian?" Craig called as he started to put on his shoes.

"For sure," Julian agreed. He always waited to see what Craig and Elliot did. Then he did the same thing.

Craig aimed his flashlight at the bunk above me. "What do you say, Raphael?"

Raphael didn't answer. All he did was jump down from his bunk and nod.

Finally Craig's flashlight beam hit me right in the eyes. "What about you, New York? Are you in—or out?"

Are you nuts? I wanted to say. Go outside in the dark? Alone? With a zombie walking around on the loose?

I looked out the window by Elliot's bunk. It was really dark. World's record dark. Something told me not even bats would go out on a night like this.

And I knew that Brian was out there— somewhere.

But what if I didn't go? What would I do? Stay in the cabin—*alone?* And just wait for Brian to come back and eat me alive?

No way, I thought. If I was going to run into a zombie, I'd rather do it with a bunch of guys at my side.

Do or die, I told myself.

"Okay, I'll go," I said finally.

"All right, New York!" Craig said with a laugh.

It was after eleven by the time we got dressed and sneaked out of our cabin. Each of us had a flashlight in one hand and a bunch of rolls of toilet paper in the other.

The ground was soaked from the evening's rain. In seconds my tennis shoes felt like sponges. I slipped and fell on some wet stones going down the hill. But I got up superfast. I wanted to be on my feet at all times…just in case I ran into *him* again.

One by one we crept around the dining hall, staying out of sight. Finally we reached Cabin 1, the first girls' cabin. It was dark and quiet inside.

This would be fun, I thought, if there wasn't a zombie in the woods. Every time I heard a footstep or a twig snap, I jumped.

It only took a few minutes to surround the cabin and drape it in toilet paper. I heaved a few rolls over the roof myself. Then I watched three rolls come over the cabin from the back. They tumbled down the pitched roof, leaving a long white paper trail behind them. Pretty quickly the cabin was a mess. It looked like a giant birthday present, decorated in white streamers.

Just as I was about to throw my last roll, I heard a sound and froze. It was a dog's cry. A long half-moan, half-wail.

That dog is either hurt or scared to death, I thought. I wondered if Brian was nearby.

Raphael was listening, too. "McDonald's pit bull," he whispered.

"What's wrong with it?" I asked.

"He just howls because he's chained up all the time," Raphael said.

"I don't think so," I said.

Two more rolls of toilet paper came over the cabin and fell at our feet.

All of a sudden, someone opened the cabin door a crack and peeked out.

"Who's there?" a girl's voice called from inside. Then the girl at the door shined a flashlight around. "It's boys!" she shouted.

"Let's get out of here!" Craig yelled.

We took off toward our cabin, as fast as we could. We sped through the woods. Then down past the dining hall. Then across the grass by the lake.

But as we started up the hill to the boys' cabins, my flashlight suddenly died. All at once, I couldn't see a thing—except the other guys' flashlights disappearing up the hill.

"Hey, wait!" I called. But they were way ahead of me. They didn't even stop or turn back.

My heart started racing.

I unscrewed the top of my flashlight to see why it died. But the top came off and the batteries fell to the ground.

Then McDonald's dog howled again.

Hey—what was that?

There was a noise up the hill ahead of me. A branch snapped. Was someone walking through the trees?

"Hey, Raphael? Craig? Elliot? Is that you?" I called in a loud whisper.

Nothing. No one answered.

I took a few steps forward but I couldn't see the path.

I heard the sound coming closer. A footstep dragging across the ground.

"Yo, guys, where are you? My flashlight's dead," I called in a trembling voice.

I sniffed a strong, stale smell in the air. Like rotten flesh. My legs started to shake. I knew what that smell was. It was Brian! He was coming to get me! But I couldn't see him yet. I didn't know which way to run.

The footsteps kept coming closer.

I had to get out of there—and fast!

I spun around and started to run back down the hill. Then I ran straight into something. Something moving and alive!

Chapter 5

"AAAHIIII!" I screamed for the second time that night. I stumbled back and fell onto the wet ground.

A flashlight snapped on, blinding me.

"I'll bet you stink at Capture the Flag," said a girl holding the flashlight. "You're easy to find."

A *girl?* How'd she get here?

But I didn't say anything. I was still listening to the footsteps. Dragging footsteps that were fading away into the woods.

"Toilet-papering our cabin," the girl went on. "Don't you know it's stupid? And childish? And bad for the environment?"

Whoa! I thought. Talk about an attitude. Right away, there was something about this girl that I liked a lot.

I squinted to see her above her flashlight beam. She was wearing an oversized red sweatshirt and jeans. The shirt made her look even thinner than she was. She had long brown hair in a tight ponytail. She was about my age—ten or eleven years old.

"Listen," I said. "Did you just hear something in the woods? Or see someone?"

"Just you," she said. "Although I'll bet there are a million bugs and animals out here. I mean, I've already counted about two hundred species of bugs I've never seen before. I hate animals. People have been teasing me about it all night."

"The kids here are jerks," I said.

"But I got teased by my *counselor*," she said. "And by some creepy girl in my cabin named Susie. She wears her hair in ugly pigtails that stick out from her head. What a creep."

She brushed her bangs away from her eyes. "What's your name?" she asked.

"Griffen. Griffen Alexander."

"Hey—that's my name, too!"

My mouth dropped open. "Your name is Griffen Alexander?" I said, standing up.

"No, silly. *Lela* Alexander. Don't you absolutely hate it here?" she went on. "I mean, where are all the Chinese restaurants? I'm starving!"

Hey, I thought. Only a New Yorker would panic if there was no Chinese restaurant in sight!

"You're from New York?" I guessed.

"Yeah," she said. "The Upper West Side. You?"

I nodded. "Same."

"So do you hate it here or what?" she said.

"Yeah," I said. But only because of the zombie wandering around in the woods, I wanted to say.

I was trying to decide whether I should tell her about Brian. But suddenly she squashed a mosquito on her leg. It left a big smear of blood.

"*Yuuuuuk.* I'm going to be eaten alive if I stay here," she said.

Eaten alive. She didn't know how right she was.

Hold it, Griffen, I thought. I couldn't tell her about the zombies. She was already too freaked out about the bugs!

"I'm going back to my cabin," she said. "But don't worry. I won't tell on you. We New Yorkers have to stick together." As she walked away, she called over her shoulder, "Go Mets."

"Go Mets," I called back.

A moment later, I was all alone again in the dark.

Now what? I thought. I still couldn't see the path. And the sounds in the trees were creepy. An owl hooted. I heard the pit bull cry again.

But finally I heard the sound I was waiting for. Voices! I saw some flashlight beams, too. Craig. Elliot. Nat. Julian.

Raphael. They were coming back!

I ran as fast as I could through the trees—straight toward their lights—until I got to them.

For a moment we just stood on a small path that led up to the boys' cabins.

"Listen," I said. I was breathing hard. "My flashlight went dead and I couldn't see. But I heard him and I smelled him. The zombie was out here. I think he was going to grab me. But then a girl ran into me and he took off."

"A *girl* chased him off?" Craig asked in disbelief. "Some zombie!"

"What a wuss," Elliot said.

"Let's get out of here," Nat said, sounding scared.

"Relax," said Elliot. "There's nothing out here. New York just heard some noises in the woods. So what? This is the great outdoors. Animals live here. Don't be a Larry. Who's for taking a rowboat out on the lake?"

"On the lake?" I said. "Hey—no way. My cousin said that's where the zombies live. Under the floating dock."

"Jeez. You don't know when to give up," said Elliot, shaking his head. "Who's coming with me?"

"Nah," said Craig. "We'd better get back to the cabin before Lance does."

"Okay, forget you guys!" said Elliot. He pushed past us. "I'm going for a swim." Then he headed down the hill to the lake by himself.

"He shouldn't do that," I said.

"Try and stop him," Craig called over his shoulder as he walked away.

The five of us hurried back to the cabin in silence. We were all sort of worried about Lance. We didn't want to get caught sneaking in.

But as we crept in through the screen door, the place seemed really empty.

"I think Lance is still at the meeting," Craig said.

"Oh, yeah? Then why's the door to his room open?" I asked.

"Hey, he's right," Raphael said. "Lance would never leave his door open. It would ruin his whole experiment."

For a minute, we all froze. We knew something was wrong. Someone had been there. Someone had been in Lance's room.

Then we started walking, slowly, in a clump, toward Lance's door. I shined my flashlight from side to side like a searchlight. But I was almost afraid to look.

"Holy Larry!" said Craig when he stepped through the door.

"Lance's zoo—it's gone!" Julian cried.

I shined my light across the space and gasped. The room was totally trashed. A lamp was knocked over. Lance's notebooks and animal cages were tossed all over the place. Every one of them was twisted out of shape. The cage doors were completely ripped off.

And the animals were missing.

"The zoo isn't gone," said Raphael. He was kneeling in one corner of the room. "At least not all of it."

I walked over to see what he meant. There on the floor were some animal pieces. Frog's legs. Part of a gecko. Mice tails. Blood all over the place.

"Oh no!" I burst out. "Something broke in here—and *ate* them all!"

Chapter 6

"What are you doing in here?"

I whirled around and saw Lance in the doorway.

He came in, sniffing the strange sick odor that filled the room. "What's wrong with my table? What happened to my cages?" The closer he got the more his face twitched. "Where are my animals?!"

I backed away fast and so did the other guys. But Lance kept walking.

He looked at one cage after another. "My animals!" he cried. Then he found what Raphael had found—the blood and the pieces.

"Oh, Newton...Jonas...Froggie," Lance mumbled. He looked like he was going to barf. I had to feel sorry for the guy.

His voice got quiet. "What happened here?"

No one said a word. So finally I spoke up.

"We don't know what happened," I said.

"You don't know?" he said angrily. "How come? You're standing right here. You sleep in the next room. Why don't you know?"

"The truth is," I said, clearing my throat, "we weren't here when it happened. We raided the girls' cabins."

"You left after lights-out?" he said. He looked really surprised. Like he couldn't believe we would break the rules.

"Sorry," I mumbled, unable to look him in the eye.

Lance's shoulders drooped. "My experiment is ruined," he said. "And my poor mice..." His voice trailed off.

"Uh, Lance," I said, "maybe we can help you clean up. Okay?"

Lance nodded and we got to work. Raphael picked up the lamp. The rest of us picked up the twisted cages. Lance had the toughest job—sweeping up what was left of his animals.

Meanwhile, I kept looking toward the door. Elliot still wasn't back from boating. Or swimming. Or whatever he was doing at the lake. I kept waiting to hear him come in. But I was afraid I'd see Brian instead.

Finally we were done. Lance gave a big sigh. "I think I know what happened here," he said. "I think a bear broke in."

"I don't think it was a bear," I said. I picked up a cage. It had some fur sticking to it.

"Why not?" Nat said.

"Because we've got enough candy and granola bars in our duffels to open up a store," I said. "A bear would've smelled that. And torn up our room to get it."

Lance thought for a moment. "Then it was probably Fritzie, McDonald's pit bull.

That thing can break free from its chains. It's vicious."

"Yeah, and we heard it wailing tonight, going crazy," Raphael said.

"Pit bulls don't pull little cages apart," I argued.

"What do *you* think it was?" Craig asked.

"I think it was a zombie," I said. "Brian. The one who was a counselor here last year."

I waited for Lance to laugh like everyone else. But instead he started nodding.

"Yeah," he said. "I've heard stories in town about this camp. They say people drown and nobody ever finds their bodies." Lance hesitated a moment before he went on. "I also heard a counselor drowned here last year."

I looked over at Craig and the other guys. Their eyes were wide. And their faces were turning pale. Like all of a sudden they knew for sure I was telling the truth.

"Right," I told Lance. "That was Brian. I saw him tonight and I almost ran into him in the woods, too."

Lance shuddered. "Hey—do you guys know how lucky you were? I mean, what if you had been here when the zombie came in?"

"Wow," said Nat. "Good thing we went on that raid!"

"We could have been like the mice," Raphael said, giving a low whistle.

Lance looked around, and then suddenly a look of fear flashed across his face.

"Go lock the cabin door," he said. "Quick."

"Good idea," Craig said. "But it doesn't lock."

"Oh, yeah," Lance said. Then he started looking at us one at a time, as if he were counting.

"Hey, wait a minute. Where's Elliot?" Lance asked, sounding worried.

Craig and I looked at each other. I

waited for him to answer.

"Uh, he's in the bathroom," Craig said.

"No, he's not," Raphael said. "He went for a swim."

"You're kidding," Lance said. He stared at us like he didn't have any idea what to do.

"So, do you think we should go look for him?" I said, glancing at the door.

"No," Lance said, shaking his head hard. The idea of going into the woods seemed to snap him awake. "I'll go tell McDonald he's gone. Let him take care of it."

Right, I thought. Except McDonald won't care. He already knows the lake is full of zombies! Why would he worry about one more missing kid?

Chapter 7

I didn't get much sleep that night. I kept seeing Brian's ugly face in the bathroom window. And those empty, twisted cages in Lance's room.

I thought I heard strange noises outside. Nearby. There were scraping sounds—kind of like someone dragging something through the woods.

He couldn't be far away. And those mice were small. He was probably still hungry.

I tried to stay awake. We all did. We were waiting for Elliot to come back. But finally we fell asleep.

The next morning, when I woke up, I looked around sleepily. Elliot's bunk was empty. No one had slept in it all night.

"Something's up with Elliot," Craig said. "Why didn't he come back?"

I didn't want to think about that.

"Let's go see if McDonald has anything to say," I said. I hopped out of bed and got dressed. Then I followed Craig and the others to the dining hall.

We got there just as McDonald walked in. "Campers, what am I doing?" he called out. He was standing at the front of the room, holding one bony hand in the air. That was the Camp Kennebec signal to get quiet. It meant McDonald wanted to talk. Like the whole world had to stop because McDonald had something to say.

I looked at my cabin mates. They nodded. We were all hoping the same thing. He was going to tell us he found Elliot. But was he alive—or dead?

McDonald cleared his throat.

"Right after breakfast, campers," McDonald said, "I want everyone to put on your swim suits. Then meet your counselors at the lake. Today we have swimming tests."

Swimming tests? Was he *crazy?* How could he send kids into *that* lake?

And what about Elliot?

I jumped up on one of the long benches next to our table. Then I cupped my hands around my mouth.

"What happened to Elliot?" I shouted at the top of my lungs. "Tell us that!"

It was amazing how fast the whole room got silent. Everyone just sort of shut up and stared at me. McDonald glared at me—like he wanted to kill me.

"What is your question, young man?" he said, trying to stay calm.

"A kid from our cabin went out last night and never came back," I said. "Elliot Patterson. I want to know if you found him yet."

McDonald cleared his throat. Then he turned and spoke to everyone in the room. "It's true—a camper has gotten lost in the woods somehow. We've called the police, and we've been looking for him since last night," McDonald said. But he sounded too calm and smiled too much.

"I'm sure we'll find him," McDonald went on. "There's no reason to think he's had an accident out by the dock."

"Hey—I never mentioned anything about him going to the dock," I said.

McDonald's face darkened. "I'll talk to you boys later," he said, glaring at me and the other guys in my cabin.

As soon as breakfast was over, all the kids ran for their cabins to change into their bathing suits. Even my cabin mates left. They weren't going into the lake—no way. But they wanted to go looking for Elliot before McDonald could stop them.

"I'm going to stay here," I told Craig. "I want to hear what McDonald has to say."

"Okay," Craig said with a nod. "But then what? What are we going to do?"

"Then I'm going to find a way to get us out of here!" I said.

I watched everyone file out of the dining hall, and waited for McDonald to come over to me. But he didn't stick around. He ran out of the room without saying a word to anyone.

Chicken, I thought. He doesn't want to face me. Maybe he knows I know the truth.

Finally the place was almost empty. I looked for a good place to sit and think. Then all of a sudden I noticed the girl I'd met in the woods last night. She was hanging around too, sitting at the far end of the dining hall.

"Not swimming?" I asked her, walking over.

"Are you kidding?" she said. She sat up on the table, pulling on her big red sweatshirt. It came over her knees. "I asked McDonald three times to show me the lake's bacteria count. He told me not to worry. The lake is safe. I said, 'Excuse me—*I'll* be the judge of that.'"

I laughed. She was tough, real tough.

"So why aren't *you* going in the water?" she asked.

I looked at her carefully. She was a girl, but I decided to trust her anyway.

"You know that guy in my cabin who's missing?" I said. "Well, I think the zombie got him."

"What zombie?" she asked without batting an eye. Like she totally believed me and just wanted to hear more about it.

"The one that's stalking this camp," I said.

It took me about ten minutes to tell her everything. About the zombies who died twenty years ago. And about the dock and the lake and the fire and everything.

Then I told her about Brian. "Last night he broke into our cabin and ate—" I stopped. I couldn't tell her about the animals. It would totally gross her out. "He ate *something* of Lance's," I said. "Anyway, I'm afraid maybe he ate Elliot, too."

She didn't say anything for a minute.

"But why didn't Brian die in the fire?" she asked finally.

I shrugged. "Maybe he's a super unkillable zombie or something."

She was quiet for a minute, but she nodded like she agreed.

"So anyway, I'm trying to figure out how to get out of here," I said. "Because I'm not going to spend another night in this place."

"No problem," Lela said. "All we have to do is call someone we trust. Someone we know will believe us."

"My parents are in Europe for three weeks," I said. "But you could call yours."

"Call my *parents?*" Lela laughed. "They'd never believe me in a million years. They'd think I was just making up a crazy story so they'd come and get me. No, silly. I meant we should call the *New York Times*."

"The *New York Times!?*" I said.

"Sure, I call them all the time," she said.

"But the *New York Times* isn't going to believe any story about zombies," I said.

"Maybe not," she said. "So we'll tell them about the drownings instead. And about Elliot disappearing. That's definitely true, right?"

I had to agree.

"Trust me," she said. "When they hear that the camp director is trying to cover up about a missing kid, they'll be up here so fast it'll make your head spin."

"It's a great plan, except for one thing," I said. "Corey told me there's only one phone. It's in Mr. McDonald's office. And he *never* lets kids use it."

"I know," she said. "A girl from my cabin got homesick the minute she got here. She broke into his office to use the phone. And guess what?"

"What?" I asked.

"There's a phone locked up in his desk drawer, all right. But it's disconnected! It doesn't even have a cord!"

"You're kidding!" I said.

"I'm not," she said. "He keeps it in there

58

just to fool us. He knows everyone wants to use his phone. But we can't. Because it doesn't even work."

"McDonald's a slime," I said. "But he's got to have a phone of some kind."

"Yup, he does," Lela answered. "I saw him use it. It's a cellular one. He keeps it in his pocket at all times."

"What a creep," I said.

"Double creep," she said.

"Okay," I said. "So there's no way to get to his phone. How are we going to get help—or get out of here?"

Lela's face got really serious.

"There's only one way I can think of," she said. "But it's dangerous. And it means we have to go near the lake."

Chapter 8

Hike around the lake to Camp Black Bear? And use *their* phone to call for help? The minute Lela said it, I knew she was right.

It was a brilliant idea. But it was also crazy. Because to get there, we had to walk through the woods.

And the woods was zombie country.

"Okay," I said, thinking fast. "I'll do it—but we have to go now. In the daytime. The zombies come out at night."

But it was after dinner by the time Lela and I got a chance to sneak away. Before that, McDonald or one of the counselors was always watching us.

Finally, around seven o'clock, we were ready to go.

"Do you think it's too late to go?" I asked her as we met at the edge of the woods.

"Why?"

"Because we've got to get over there, make the calls, and get back before it gets dark," I said. "Otherwise…"

"No problem," Lela said. "Their camp isn't that far away." But she sounded nervous and checked her watch.

How far is it? I wondered. I mean, the lake wasn't very wide—but it was long. And we had to go all the way around one end of the hot dog bun.

"Watch out for bugs," Lela warned me as we followed the path.

Bugs? I thought. They're the least of our problems!

Finally, about forty minutes later, we began to hear boys shouting.

We crept up to the edge of the woods. We watched a bunch of guys playing Ultimate Frisbee in the clearing.

"Hey—look," I said. "Normal kids, having normal fun."

Lela nodded, with a sad look on her face.

We stared at Camp Black Bear for a minute. It was totally different from our camp. The cabins looked cozy and had fresh paint. There was a ring of Native American tepees set up. I even heard horses whinnying not far away. Cool place, I thought. I had forgotten that camp was supposed to be fun.

"There's the main office," Lela said, pointing to a dark red building about fifty feet away. "I bet we'll find a phone in there."

"Okay," I said. Then I took off my Mets cap and gave it to her. "Here. Hide your hair."

"How come?" she asked.

"Because this is a *boys'* camp," I said. "I think they'll notice that you're a girl."

While Lela tucked her hair under the

cap, I shook my shoulders to loosen up. I wanted to act natural. Like I belonged at Camp Black Bear.

Do or die, Griffen, I told myself as we walked to the office door.

The small building had a front porch with two steps. Then a screen door and a big wooden door standing wide open.

We walked right in the front door like we owned the place.

Bingo! The office was empty! And there was a phone, sitting right in the middle of the desk.

"Come on—let's go for it!" I said.

Lela ran right to the phone and started dialing. She knew the number by heart. I guess she wasn't kidding when she said she called the *New York Times* a lot.

Pretty soon she started talking fast. "Hello, Sara Richmond? This is Lela Alexander. I'm at Camp Kennebec in Maine. You'd better come up here right away. Something terrible is happening. A kid has disappeared. Lots of people have drowned. And the camp director won't do anything about it! I think there's a good story here. You've got to check it out. Thanks. See you soon. Bye."

"Is she coming?" I asked.

Lela hung up. "I don't know. I got her voice mail," she said, looking disappointed.

I stepped around to the back of the desk. "Okay. Me next."

"Who are you calling?" she asked. "I thought your parents were away."

"They are," I said. "But I just remembered my grandparents. They live about a hundred miles from here."

"A hundred miles?" Lela said, slapping her head. "Why didn't you say so before? They could get here fast!"

"Yeah," I said. I listened to the phone. "It's ringing forever."

Finally a friendly voice answered.

"Hello…"

"Hi, Grandma. It's Griffen," I said.

"You have reached the answering machine of George and Martha Alexander. Please leave a message after the beep."

"Oh no," I said. "They aren't home!"

I waited for the beep. Then I said, "Hi, Grams. This is Griffen. Listen, I really need your help. I'm at Camp Kennebec—but it's really Camp Harvest Moon. It's the same camp Corey and Amanda went to last summer. And it's full of zombies! I'm not kidding. Come get me. Please! Bye."

"Great!" Lela said. "Now someone will come and rescue us."

"Don't count on it," I said gloomily. "My grandparents have a new RV. They like to take long trips. They could be gone for weeks."

"Oh," Lela said.

Yeah, I thought. So much for finding a phone. No one was going to rescue us.

I looked at Lela's watch.

"Hey—it's getting late. We'd better hurry. It'll be dark soon."

We ran out the front door of the office. A few fireflies blinked in front of us. The sun was already going down.

"I brought a flashlight," Lela said.

"Me, too," I said as we ducked into the woods.

The path around the lake was already pretty dark. And by the time we'd been walking for twenty minutes, it was pitch black.

Big mistake.

I shined my flashlight ahead of us. What happened to the woods? I wondered. The trees all looked so much taller and closer together. Everything sounded louder. Frogs and crickets seemed to be calling out a warning.

But my heart pounding was the loudest sound of all.

We walked as fast as we could. We didn't talk much.

A branch moved and an owl screeched. Lela stopped and grabbed my arm.

"Let's go back. Back to Camp Black Bear," she said.

"We can't," I said. "We've gone too far. I mean, I think if we just keep going…"

Suddenly a twig snapped.

What was that?

Something was out there, in the bushes

McDonald's pit bull started howling in the distance.

And then all at once, with a powerful swishing sound, the bushes parted.

"No!" I screamed. "It's him!" I couldn't move—and I couldn't look away.

In my flashlight beam, I saw a loose, fleshy body in mud-caked clothes. Brian was walking stiffly toward me with his arms stretched straight out in front of him and his mouth hanging open.

Then as he moved toward me, I saw something even worse. There was another zombie coming through the bushes. And I knew who it was.

It was Elliot!

Chapter 9

I wanted to scream at the top of my lungs. But I couldn't. My vocal cords were frozen.

Don't kill me! That's all I could think as I stared at Elliot's half-dead body in front of me.

He was more disgusting than I ever could have imagined. His glasses were broken and muddy. His pale face was so white it looked like he'd been dead for years. There was a piece of seaweed in his dark hair. Water dripped from his forehead into his eyes.

The worst part was his eyes. His *dead* eyes—just like Brian's. They never closed. Never blinked. Even when the water dripped into them.

Elliot's arms were stretched out straight in front of him. He and Brian were both coming toward us—thin hands ready to grab.

Elliot turned toward Lela, then toward me. As if he were making a choice. Then, with a lurch, he suddenly grabbed her!

Lela let out a scream so loud and deep, I thought I felt the ground shake. A moment later, Brian started coming toward me.

My heart pounded so hard I thought I'd choke.

I wanted to yell, "Run! Lela! Run!" But nothing came out.

She pulled away from Elliot and started running anyway, like a maniac. She tore into the woods and disappeared, with him walking stiffly after her.

I tried to follow her but my foot got tangled in a tree root. I fell flat on my face and hit the ground hard.

Get up, Griffen. *Get up!* I told myself as I caught a sudden whiff of the zombies' gross rotten death smell.

As I looked over my shoulder, I saw Brian closing in on me. He towered over me, just a few feet away.

And he was holding something in his right hand. It looked like a club.

What's that? I wondered, squinting hard in the darkness.

Before I could move, he raised his stiff arm over his head and hurled the thing at me!

I ducked and heard it hit the tree a few feet away. In my flashlight beam I saw the bloody leg bone of an animal!

It was almost eaten clean. Only a few small clumps of raw flesh were left.

Stumbling, I jumped to my feet and darted forward.

Let me get away, I prayed.

But two powerful hands grabbed me in the darkness. I turned around and saw the pale, bloated face under the Raiders cap. It was white with death.

"Help!" I finally screamed—just as he closed his fingers around my neck.

I dropped my flashlight and tried to pry his hands loose. But he was too strong. Inhumanly strong. I kicked at his legs and punched his face wildly.

Nothing stopped him. His hands were slowly pulling me closer and closer to his open mouth. The smell of rotten flesh blew into my nose.

I'm going to die, I thought.

THWAAACK!

The loud thump came out of nowhere. Then Brian lurched forward. He was about to fall on me! I dodged to one side, and he fell to the ground.

What had happened? In the darkness, I couldn't tell where I was. I bent over and picked up my flashlight.

"Lela?" She was standing there holding a branch about as thick as her arm. Somehow she'd gotten away from Elliot. She'd come back!

"Griffen, are you okay?" she cried, her voice trembling.

I couldn't answer her. I just wanted to get out of there. But when I tried to run, something grabbed my leg!

It was Brian! His two strong hands tightened around my left ankle.

I grabbed the branch from Lela and gave him another whack.

The instant he let go, I started to run. Lela followed me.

"Which way do we go?" she yelled.

How would I know? We were off the path. Brian was coming. And Elliot was probably nearby. I could hear someone dragging himself through the woods just a few feet away.

Then all of a sudden Lela shined her flashlight through the trees—and there was Elliot! Only three feet away!

He was still walking stiffly, trampling bushes and everything else in his path. I knew he would never get tired. Never stop.

And the rotten stink of his zombie flesh was awful.

"Run, Griffen!" Lela shouted. "Don't let him grab you. He's too strong!"

I turned in circles for a moment, terrified and confused.

Then I saw the lights in the distance. Camp Kennebec lights.

We ran as hard as we could. The footsteps kept following us. Slow footsteps dragging through the bushes.

I didn't look back this time. I just kept moving, running toward the lights. When we finally got there, we saw that it wasn't just the cabins. It was a fire, a campfire.

"We made it," I said, almost too exhausted to run another step.

We got there just as the whole camp were gathering around. They were singing some stupid song about sleeping under the stars.

A campfire blazed in the middle of the big circle. They didn't know how lucky they were to have that fire.

I found Lance as fast as I could. He was standing with the guys from Cabin 5. I pulled him away from the group.

"We saw him. We found Elliot," I said, still panting for breath.

"Where?"

"In the woods. It was horrible. He's a zombie!" I said.

"Oh no," Lance said, his eyes opening wide with fear. "No!"

"We've got to do something. Call his parents. Call the police," I said, talking fast.

"Right," Lance nodded. Then he went into his scientist mode. "But how did he turn into a zombie?"

"Who knows?" I said. "All I know is something in the lake makes it happen."

Lance glanced nervously toward the woods.

"They're out there right now," I said. "Brian and Elliot. And who knows how many others there are? Do you have a car?

Because we've got to get out of here fast!"

Lance frowned. "No," he said. "I never learned to drive."

Out of the corner of my eye, I saw Mr. McDonald coming toward us.

"Griffen, Lela," he said sternly, "did I just see you coming out of the woods? Where have you been?"

"We went over to Camp Black Bear," I said, blurting out the truth. I didn't care how mad McDonald got. He had to know the truth. "On the way back we were chased by two zombies. And one of them was Elliot!"

"He tried to bite my *face*," Lela said. She made it sound like it was all McDonald's fault.

McDonald shook his head. "We have a rule about hiking alone in the woods. And you know it."

"Who cares about your stupid rules? Didn't you hear us? There's something in the woods that eats flesh and won't die!" I shouted. "The zombies are going to get us!"

McDonald glared at me.

"If you hadn't broken the rule, you could sit around the fire and tell this silly ghost story," he said. "But instead I'm going to send you to your cabin. Make that both of you."

"Oh, great. We'll just sit there and be zombie bait," Lela said.

"You'll stay there all day tomorrow, too," McDonald went on. "Including when we go over to Camp Black Bear for a cookout."

"A cookout?" I said. "Oh, great. What's for dinner? Cabin 2?"

I didn't give McDonald a chance to yell at me again. I went back to my cabin, all right. I went back there and packed!

Just in case my grandparents showed up.

But after I packed, I was so tired I fell asleep—even before my cabin mates returned.

By the time I woke up, it was almost noon the next day. The cabin was empty.

Except there was a note from Craig. It said, "Lance told us about the zombies—and about Elliot. Nat puked when he heard. And Julian started crying for his mom. But I won't believe it until I hear it from you. This camp sure is *the worst*.

"Anyway, sorry you got grounded. I'm going to try to sneak in and use the phone at Camp Black Bear like you did. Because someone has got to come and get us out of here! I'll call Elliot's parents, too.

"Wish me luck. See you tonight after the cookout. Craig."

Don't do it, Craig, I thought. Don't go wandering around in the woods alone. Especially not now.

Not with Brian and your good buddy Elliot on the loose!

Chapter 10

For the rest of the afternoon, I sat on my bunk. I was worrying about Craig. And praying my grandparents would arrive. But after six hours, no one showed up.

Bummer, I thought. Craig and I were just starting to be friends. And now he's probably being eaten by a zombie.

I got more freaked out just before sunset. That's when the whole camp got into canoes and paddled across the lake. They were going to the cookout. And then when it got dark, the counselors were going to set off fireworks from the floating dock in the middle of the lake.

As the sun went down, the wind picked up. Sometimes it blew the smell of charcoal and hamburgers across the lake.

But sometimes it blew something rotten. The sickening smell of rotting flesh.

Were the zombies over there? Hiding in the bushes? Or were they here, in our camp?

I wondered if Craig had made it to the phone. And if Lela was all right. She must be all alone in her cabin, too.

Hey—nobody was stopping me from finding out! Besides, I couldn't stay there by myself one more second.

I ran out of my cabin and down the hill. The whole camp was empty and silent. "Yo! Prisoner Number Two!" I called out when I got to her cabin.

"Hi," Lela said, stepping out the door.

"Let's raid the dining hall. What do you say?" I said.

She gave me a thumbs-up and followed me to the dining hall.

After we went in, I locked the door behind us. For a few minutes, we tried having some fun. We made jokes about what we'd do if we got turned into zombies.

I said I'd terrorize McDonald and his dumb dog. Lela said she'd like to get back at her counselor for teasing her so much about the bugs.

We found some cupcakes and scarfed them down, sitting on the dining hall tables.

But then we glanced at the window. The trees outside seemed too tall and too dark. And suddenly the dining hall seemed too empty. My heart began to pound.

"It's creepy in here," I said, staring at the light of a fire across the lake.

"Yeah," Lela said with a shiver.

"My grandparents didn't come," I said.

"The *New York Times* didn't either," she said. "Are you scared?"

Before I could answer, a loud noise made me jump to my feet.

It was the sound of a creaky door opening behind us.

I turned around, but no one was standing there.

ARFF! ARFF-ARFF-ARFF!

Suddenly McDonald's crazy pit bull charged toward us.

"What's he doing in here?" Lela screamed, backing away.

"I don't know," I yelled. "I thought he was chained up!"

As the dog raced toward me, I stumbled over a table, trying to get away. The pit bull was snarling. His teeth were snapping. He looked like he wanted to kill someone!

In the next instant, the dog ran straight past us—all the way to the front door.

"Look! He's not trying to attack us. He's after *him!*" Lela shouted as the dog barked and growled.

In the moonlight, I saw a tall figure standing there. Peering through the window in the door.

Oh, no! I thought when I saw the gray, spongy face.

It was Brian. And he was trying to get in!

Chapter 11

He can see me, I thought. I'm in clear view, and he can see me.

Brian pressed his face close to the door. It was a dark, blank shadow hidden under his Raiders cap.

He knows I'm afraid, I thought.

But I couldn't run. I was frozen. Trembling. Just staring at him. He seemed even bigger and stronger than he had in the woods.

That sick feeling in my stomach came back—the same feeling I had the moment I arrived at Camp Zombie.

I knew what it was. A warning—of my own death.

"What do we do, Griffen?" Lela asked,

her voice shaking. She was right next to me, almost shouting because the dog was barking so loud.

Do? What *could* we do against a creature that was strong enough to rip the legs off an animal?

With a crash, the door suddenly flew into a million pieces of wood and glass. And he was coming right toward us!

His stiff arms stuck out in front of him—like they were dangling on invisible ropes.

"Come on!" I yelled at Lela. I almost tripped and fell, trying to get away.

We ran halfway down the aisle between two rows of tables. I slid to a stop at the back door of the dining hall. Lela was right behind me. I grabbed the door handle and yanked it open.

"AAAHIIII!" Lela screamed at the top of her lungs.

Standing there at the back door was another zombie—a kid. But it wasn't Elliot! It was a girl!

The girl had the same dead eyes as Elliot and Brian. And her face was just as gray. There was seaweed in her hair, tangled in with her pigtails. They stuck straight out from both sides of her head.

Then I noticed she was wearing a gold necklace. It had her name written on it in script. SUSIE.

"AAAHIIII!" Lela screamed again as she stomped on Susie's feet. I looked down and saw the pink glow-in-the-dark laces on her sneakers.

No! I felt like screaming. Not another one. Not another zombie.

But I knew it was true. Why not? Lots of kids swam out to the floating dock. And I knew there was something terrible in that lake. Something that turned people into zombies!

Suddenly the girl reached out to get me. She just put one hand on my neck and pulled me toward her. Her grip was so powerful, I couldn't breathe. My legs wobbled. Her rotten stench filled my nose.

I'm dead meat, I thought. Dead meat.

I closed my eyes and prayed that I'd pass out.

But the sound of Lela screaming in my ear made me open my eyes again.

No! I wanted to yell. But I couldn't speak. Another zombie was coming toward us!

Elliot walked stiffly through the back door, like nothing could stop him. A zombie with a mission.

Do something, Griffen, I told myself. Do or *die!*

With all my might, I reached out and pushed Susie away from me. At the same time, I kicked her in the stomach. She didn't even flinch, but my kick made her let go.

Then Lela and I turned and ran.

We might just make it, I thought as we stumbled forward. Only one small problem. We were headed straight toward Brian!

He dragged his feet along the wooden floor, like a machine with no OFF button. He was really close now.

"We're trapped!" I screamed over the sound of the pit bull's barking.

ARFF! ARFF! ARFF!

Then, suddenly, out of the darkness, the dog leaped through the air. Growling viciously, he attacked Brian from behind! He took a bite out of Brian's gray, spongy neck!

Brian spun and flailed wildly, trying to shake the dog off. It gave Lela and me time to make a dash for it.

We split up. She took off down the left side of the dining hall. I dodged to the right and dashed down the other side. We were both heading toward the door by the lake—the only way out.

"Griffen!" Lela called. She was standing in what was left of the doorway. "The lake!"

No, I thought. It can't be. Don't tell me more zombies are coming. I felt dizzy at the thought. I couldn't bear it.

"It's a boat! A motorboat. Someone's coming!" she shouted. "Let's run for it!"

"Great idea!" I yelled. I took a short cut, leaping over a table to get to the door.

Outside, I sucked in as much crisp air as I could. I had to get the stench of the zombies out of my lungs.

Then Lela and I ran all the way to the lake. As I looked for the boat she had seen, the sky turned colors above us. Green first, then silver, bright as daylight. The first of the fireworks had been launched from the floating dock.

The burst of light lit up the lake. I saw a small motorboat moving toward shore. It had only one person in it—a stick figure in the back of an aluminum boat. "It's Mr. McDonald!" I wanted to cheer. "Come on, McDonald! Hurry! Get us out of here!"

When the boat hit shore, he jumped out and ran toward us.

"I hear Fritzie barking," he said, striding

right past us. "What's wrong? What did you do to him?"

Lela and I hurried to keep up. He was heading for the dining hall.

"We didn't do anything," I said. "It was Brian!"

McDonald ignored me. "Fritzie! Here, boy! Here Fritzie!"

"Don't go in! They're in there!" Lela warned McDonald. "He broke the door down to get us!"

"You must have made him angry," McDonald said.

"No, not your *dog!*" I said. "The zombie!"

"Fritzie! Here, boy! Daddy's here!"

It was too late. McDonald wouldn't listen, and there was nothing we could do to stop him. He stormed into the dining hall. Lela and I backed away, down the hill toward the water.

Then I heard a scream like nothing I'd ever heard before in my life.

"Oh no," Lela gasped.

They got him, I said to myself. I thought I was going to throw up. Even McDonald didn't deserve to be eaten alive.

But a minute later McDonald came running out of the dining hall. Fritzie trotted at his side.

McDonald's face was white with horror and fear. I could tell he wasn't thinking. He just kept on running—terrified for his life.

The zombies were right behind him. They took long steps with their stiff legs.

I wondered if Brian had bitten him. Or Elliot. Or Susie!

Just then another rocket went off. They were shooting them off about every fifteen seconds. Mr. McDonald and his dog looked blood red in the light of the fireworks as they jumped into the little motorboat. The zombies were only a couple of feet behind.

"Go, go!" I chanted as McDonald started the motor. "Get out of here. Fast!"

Then it hit me. What was I thinking?

The water? The dock? That was the worst possible place McDonald could go!

"Wait!" I shouted. "Stop!"

But he couldn't hear me. My voice was drowned out by the roar of the motor. McDonald moved away from the shore at full speed, just as Brian, Elliot, and Susie reached the water.

The monsters kept walking into the water. Now it was almost to their knees. Lela and I watched as they stood still for a second.

Weird, I thought. What are they doing?

Then all at once, they sank straight down. It was as if they were in an elevator and had pushed the DOWN button. They just melted into the water.

"Did you see that?" asked Lela. "Where'd they go? How'd they do that?"

"I don't know," I said.

As the fireworks continued to go off, the motorboat, with McDonald and Fritzie aboard, sped away. At first he seemed to be heading toward the other camp. But then he turned and steered toward the floating dock.

"No, not there," I said.

Just then, I heard the motor cut off. It was too dark to tell what was going on.

"Did he make it?" Lela asked.

"I can't tell," I said.

It seemed like forever until the next fireworks were launched. When they exploded, I saw McDonald and the little boat. He was pulled up near the dock.

Then all of a sudden, the boat flipped all the way over.

"What happened?" Lela asked. "How can a rowboat tip over like that?"

I couldn't answer her. I couldn't even look. I knew if I did, the boat would be empty. And McDonald and Fritzie would be gone.

"Come on, Lela," I said. "We'd better run."

"Wait. I want to make sure they reach

the dock," she said.

"Don't hold your breath," I said.

"What do you mean? Where are they?"

Before I could tell her, a figure suddenly rose up out of the lake. He glided straight up as smoothly as he had glided down. And he was only a few feet away from us.

Dripping with seaweed and water, Brian reached out his arms and started walking.

Lela and I both screamed.

Chapter 12

"Help! Somebody help us!" I yelled until my lungs hurt. I kept calling to the people across the lake. There were hundreds of kids and counselors over there. Plus the counselors on the dock who were setting off the fireworks. We only needed one of them to hear us.

"Help!" Lela shouted, backing away from the lake and from Brian.

As fireworks brightened the sky with color, I got a good look at Brian's expressionless face. For an instant I thought I saw my face. Was that going to be me? Dead. No voice. No thoughts. Skin falling off in clumps. Killing one thing after another.

"HELP!" I yelled.

"They can't hear us," Lela said, dragging me away from the lake. "The fireworks are too loud."

I knew she was right. It was time to face the truth. No one was going to come. We were going to die alone.

"We've got to run for it!" I yelled.

Lela and I started running away from the lake. But where could we go? The dining hall? No, that place was a trap.

I couldn't think of any place where Brian wouldn't follow us. So I headed for Cabin 5—because I didn't know where else to go.

As soon as we reached the cabin, I snapped off the lights. "Let's hide under the beds," I said, my voice shaking. In the dark, I squeezed under one of the bunks. Lela crawled under another.

"Griffen, do you have any matches? A lighter?" she said. "I mean, why didn't they tell us what we really needed to pack for this lousy camp?"

I knew she was joking so she wouldn't

feel scared to death. But I didn't want to answer. I didn't want Brian to hear us.

"Shhh," I said.

"Are we safe here?" she asked softly from the other side of the room.

Are we safe anywhere? I wondered. Then I remembered something. Something that almost made me scream. Cabin 5 was Brian's cabin last year! Corey said he hated it—and everyone in it! This was the worst place in the world to hide!

Suddenly there was a loud thud. Someone had blasted the door right off its hinges. It fell to the floor with a crash.

I peeked out from under the bed. He was standing in the room. My throat tightened with pure fear.

Brian's feet dragged like sandpaper across the floor toward my bunk. Closer. Closer. Closer. We were trapped—just waiting to be eaten.

My heart felt like it was going to explode. There was no way I could stay there one second longer.

I pushed myself out from under the bunk and bumped right into Brian's legs. But I scrambled up as fast as I could. Then I ran straight into Lance's room.

I didn't have to look back to know Brian was following me.

I hope this works, I thought. Or else I've just trapped myself in my own grave.

I hurried to the window in Lance's room. It had a screen in it. I gave the screen a push, but it didn't budge. It was painted shut or something.

The smell of the zombie flesh was getting stronger.

"Close the door!" I shouted to Lela. "Close the door and lock us in!"

I heard her scramble out from under her bed. Then I heard heavy metal trunks being pushed across the floor.

She had blocked the door with trunks.

I forced myself to turn around for just a second—to see where Brian was. He was moving toward me like a robot. Another few seconds and…

I took a deep breath. It was now or never. I jumped up and gave the screen a kick.

It worked! The screen popped out of the window and dropped to the ground.

"AAAHIIII!" I shouted, diving out the window head first.

The ground was pretty rocky but there were enough pine needles to cushion my fall. Quickly I jumped up and looked back at the window. Brian was standing there, getting ready to climb out.

My heart pounded as I stared up at the heavy wooden shutter that hung over the open window. It wasn't a regular shutter. Just a big heavy board on hinges. When it was open, it was hooked up with an old rusty chain.

I knew if I could just unhook it, it would come crashing down.

Come on, Griffen. Do or DIE!

I leaped up and punched the heavy

wooden board with all my might. The hook moved and the chain came loose. An instant later, the shutter dropped down with a loud bang.

Yes! I thought as I watched it smack Brian right in the face. I heard him fall back into the cabin, onto the floor.

Just then Lela came running around the cabin.

"Are you okay?" she cried.

"Yeah!" I started to say.

But all at once I heard something that made me look up. The fireworks grand finale was starting.

"Listen," I said.

"What is it?"

"Whistling," I said.

A single rocket whistled into the air. Right over our heads. It sounded way too close. I looked up into the trees overhead. A trail of sparks! One of the rockets was coming our way!

"Let's get out of here!" I said.

We darted away from the cabin and dove into the woods. Just as we hit the ground, the rocket landed where we had been standing. It exploded into streaks of color and light. The whole building seemed to turn blue and green—and then yellow.

Yellow flame.

"Look," I said. "The pine needles are catching fire!"

Lela and I hurried to get farther away. Then we watched as the fire spread from the pine needles to the cabin itself. The old building caught fire fast. In seconds Lance's room went up in flames.

For just a moment, I thought I saw the heavy shutter bounce. It seemed like Brian was fighting like a madman to push it open—to get out.

But as the flames grew, the bouncing stopped.

Then I knew it was over. Brian the zombie had finally joined the world of the *dead*.

Chapter 13

Maybe we should have danced and cheered. But Lela and I didn't say a word. We just walked down the hill to the lake.

We got there in time to see one last rocket light up the sky. Then I looked back at Cabin 5. It was still burning.

"At least we got rid of Brian," I said.

But we both knew that it wasn't enough. Susie and Elliot were still out there.

The gang across the lake must have noticed the cabin burning, because pretty soon everyone came hurrying back in boats and canoes. The police came and so did the fire department. But they were too late. Cabin 5 had burned to the ground.

While everyone watched, Lance and my

cabin mates came up to me and Lela. I was happy to see Craig. I had been worried about him all day.

Lance and the others took us aside.

"What happened?" Lance asked.

"They're going to find a body in that cabin," Lela said.

Lance looked startled. And I saw Craig's face go pale.

"It's not Elliot," I said quickly. "It's Brian. We trapped him in his old room—your room, Lance. Then the fireworks hit the cabin."

Julian looked upset. "But what about…"

He didn't finish his question, but I knew what he meant.

"We didn't get Elliot," I said. "He and Susie are still out there."

"Susie?" Lance and Craig both asked at the same time.

Quickly I told them about the girl zombie. And how she and Elliot sank into the lake.

"Wow," Lance said. "No wonder McDonald's boat went down so fast."

"Did you see it?" I asked, surprised.

"Yeah," Lance said, nodding. "I was out on the dock helping with the fireworks. I saw McDonald's boat go over. But his body never came to the top."

I wasn't surprised—but still it made me feel sick. I knew McDonald and Fritzie weren't dead *or* alive now.

A little later, Lela and I had to tell the police our story—but we left out the part about the zombies. Why bother? They wouldn't believe us anyway.

Then the counselors called a meeting to tell us what would happen next. They said everyone's parents would be called in the morning. The camp was going to close because of Susie's and Elliot's disappearances and McDonald's drowning.

"Tonight," announced one of the counselors, "is your last night at Camp Kennebec. Everyone go to your cabins. Except

Cabin 5. You guys can camp out on the shore of the lake."

"No way," Craig said.

For a minute I thought the other counselors were going to give us trouble.

But all of a sudden, Lance took charge. He came through with a really great idea. "Let's build a huge bonfire in the clearing and burn it all night," he said. "Cabin 5 will camp there. And anyone else who wants to join us."

So that's what we did. We piled the bonfire high with papers, rags, sticks, and leaves. And then I ran into McDonald's office and brought out all of the Camp Kennebec brochures I could find. We took turns throwing them on the fire. They kept the fire burning really well.

Then we all sat around the blazing fire and kept our eyes on the lake.

But late that night, some of the guys fell asleep. Lance, Craig, Lela, and I were the only ones awake.

We knew it was our last night together. We'd be going home in the morning. And believe it or not, I think we were all feeling a little sad.

"You know," I said to Craig. "I'm thinking of rooting for the White Sox from now on. After the Mets, of course."

"Not me," Craig said. "I'm thinking maybe I'll take a look at the Cubs. I mean, it wouldn't kill me to root for a National League team."

"The Cubs?" I said. "They're the *Larryest* team in the universe!"

"So what, Griffen?" Craig said with a smile.

Griffen. It sounded good, coming from him. It was the first time he'd called me by my real name.

"Hey—my friends call me New York," I said, smiling back. Then I threw another stick in the bonfire. "By the way," I said to him. "There's something I've got to know."

"What?" Craig said.

"Who the heck is Larry?" I asked.

Craig laughed. "It's Nat's fat old dog. He smells worse than a zombie," he said, laughing some more.

We could hardly keep our eyes open by the time morning came. But as the sun came up, I started to feel really happy. Like maybe we really would be home soon—and life would go back to normal.

And now that it was almost daylight, I felt safe.

"Maybe we can do stuff together when we get back to New York," I said to Lela. She was still wide awake, sitting near the dying embers of the fire.

"I'm getting a tetanus booster shot first thing when I get home," she said. "You should, too."

"I'll think about it," I said with a smile. "Go Mets."

"Go Mets," said Lela.

After that, I looked out toward the lake. The sun was just rising on the far side. Its pale light cast an eerie glow over the water.

Good-bye, lake, I thought. I won't miss you for a minute.

Then I stood up and swallowed hard. What was that in the distance?

Was someone in the water?

No. Not someone. There were four of them.

A tall thin man, a short dog, and two kids. They all walked stiffly—and the man's arms were stretched out straight in front of him. As if they were suspended by invisible ropes.

Not now! I thought. They can't come out in the daytime—can they?

I watched them all walk straight out of the water and disappear into the shadowy woods.

Then a horrible chill ran down my spine, as I realized the truth. This wasn't the end. It was just the beginning. Now McDonald had his own zombie camp—a camp for the living dead!

Megan Stine and H. William Stine have written more than sixty books together. Among them are many mystery, adventure, and humor titles for young readers. The Stines have lived all across the country, from San Francisco to New York City. They presently live in Atlanta, Georgia, with their thirteen-year-old son, Cody. Every once in a while, when the moon is right, the Stines think about opening a summer camp in Maine—but they haven't quite found the right lake yet.